REAL TALK BEFORE HIGH SCHOOL

Created by Youth from Newark, NJ and Gary, IN

Edited by Joy Lindsay Mayes

Published by

Butterfly Dreamz®

ISBN: 978-0-9961070-5-1

How to Read This Book

This book is part story, part podcast, part group chat, part advice column. You will see:

- **Chapter scenes:** short bits of what Tee, Justin, or Olivia is living through.
- **Podcast letters:** real-feeling notes from classmates sent to the show.
- **Peer responses:** a friend's reply—written by youth in Newark, NJ and Gary, IN.
- **Real Talk Takeaway boxes:** the one thing you can carry into the hallway tomorrow.
- **Try This prompts:** small things to write, draw, or notice this week.
- **Group chat snippets:** how Tee, Justin, and Olivia actually talk to each other.
- **Reflection questions:** at the end of each chapter, you'll find a few questions to think about on your own or talk through with a group. You can write your answers in a journal, discuss them in class, or just let them sit in your head for a while. There are no wrong answers. The point is to notice what comes up for you.

♥ A note about the hard stuff

Some letters in this book talk about people being mean, controlling, or unsafe.

If anything in here feels like your real life, please talk to a trusted adult—a parent, grandparent, auntie, uncle, teacher, coach, counselor, librarian, or anyone you trust.

You do not have to handle a scary or unsafe relationship alone. Real help is real love.

🎙 Meet the Real Talk Crew

Tee

Taneka—but call her Tee. Honor roll, cheer captain in training, debate team. Loves a clipboard and a plan. Warm, ambitious, sometimes too much in her head. Her dream is to get into Greenway Magnet on the other side of the city.

Justin

Justin is funny, honest, and a little guarded. He loves gaming and beats. He watches his little brother Marcus after school so his mom can pick up shifts. He wants to retire his mom one day. He keeps the crew real.

Olivia

Olivia is from Ecuador and has been in the U.S. since fifth grade. She draws everywhere—notebooks, napkins, the inside of her sneakers. She's warm, free, and quick to laugh. Sometimes a phrase slides out in Spanish (don't worry, she translates).

Chapter 1

The Idea That Wouldn't Leave Me Alone

narrated by Tee

Okay, real talk. The idea for the podcast did not come from me. It came from a flyer.

A flyer. Taped crooked to the bulletin board outside the main office. The kind of flyer most kids walk past while typing in their phones. But I saw it. I always see them.

The flyer said: NATIONAL STUDENT PODCAST CONTEST. TEN THOUSAND DOLLAR GRAND PRIZE. SHOW US A SHOW. The letters were all caps, like the flyer was already yelling at me.

Ten thousand dollars. Split three ways, that is more than three thousand each. Three thousand dollars could buy a laptop that does not freeze when I try to open more than two tabs. It could buy Olivia real art supplies. It could give Justin a month where he does not have to pick up grocery store hours after watching his brother. I started doing the math in the hallway like a weirdo.

By third period I had a name in my notebook: ***Real Talk Podcast***. Honest. Short. Eighth graders saying the things eighth graders never get to say.

```
— group chat: REAL TALK CREW —
Tee: okay don’t laugh
Tee: i think we should enter a podcast contest
Justin: lol who is we
Tee: you me olivia. 10K split 3 ways.
```

Olivia: wait wait wait. dime más. tell me more 👀

Justin: three thousand each? i'm listening.

I knew this would only work if the show was about something we actually cared about. Not "tips for studying." Not "how to be popular." Something real.

I kept thinking about Kayla. My old best friend. We used to walk to school together every single day in fifth grade. She joined volleyball last year and now she leaves me on read for three days at a time. In the hallway her eyes slide over me like I'm a locker.

I wasn't the only one. Everywhere I looked, kids were dealing with something messy and pretending they weren't. Friend groups breaking. People dating people they were scared of. Brothers and sisters being mean in front of company. So much of it nobody talked about out loud.

So we wouldn't just talk. We would let our classmates write in. Letters, anonymous, sent to a podcast email. Letters about the stuff that actually hurts. And we would respond, the three of us, in three different voices.

Mom signed the permission form at 9:47 p.m. with a tired half-smile. She said, "Just don't blow up at school."

I laughed. I should not have laughed.

🎙 Real Talk Takeaway

A good idea doesn't have to be loud or fancy. Sometimes it's just a name in a notebook.

If something hurts that nobody is talking about, that is probably a thing worth saying out loud, with care.

💡 Try This Sometime This Week

Open a notes app. Write down one thing you wish someone would say out loud at your school. You don't have to share it. Just notice that you wrote it.

Chapter 1 Reflection Questions

1) Tee says she always notices flyers that other kids walk past. What is something you notice that most people around you seem to miss?

2) The podcast idea came from pain—Tee thinking about Kayla leaving her on read. Have you ever turned something that hurt into something creative or useful? What did that feel like?

3) Tee describes seeing kids *"dealing with something messy and pretending they weren't."* Why do you think people pretend everything is fine even when it isn't?

4) **Your Turn:** Write down one thing you wish someone would say out loud at your school. You don't have to share it; just notice that it matters enough to write.

NATIONAL
STUDENT
PODCAST
CONTEST
!!!
TEN THOUSAND
DOLLAR
GRAND PRIZE
SHOW US
A SHOW.
drawn by
Olivia

Chapter 2

Why I Said Yes

narrated by Justin

I'm going to be honest. When Tee said "podcast," I almost said no.

It's not that I don't talk. I talk. I just don't love hearing my own voice played back at me. There is something weird about how you sound from the inside compared to outside.

But here is the math. Three thousand dollars. My mom works two jobs. She's tired in a way I don't know how to describe except that even her smile looks tired. If I won three thousand dollars, that's legit groceries. That's no "we'll figure it out" for at least a few months.

And my little brother Marcus is six and obsessed with everything I do. If big brother is on a podcast, then in his world, big brother is famous. That's worth something too.

So I said yes. I also said I would only do it if we kept it real. No fake voice. No fake hosts. If I think a letter sounds like nonsense, I get to say it sounds like nonsense. With respect, but for real.

Tee said, "Justin, that is literally the whole point."

Olivia drew a little microphone in the corner of my math notebook and added wings on it. She labeled it "Mariposa Mic." Mariposa means butterfly. She doesn't know it yet, but I'm keeping that notebook forever.

— group chat: REAL TALK CREW —

Justin: okay i'm in. but i get to say what i think.

Tee: YES that is literally the format

Olivia: i can do the cover art!!!! con todo!!!

Justin: translation pls

Olivia: "with everything." aka all my love.

The first letter came in a week later. The subject line said "Invisible in the Hallway." I opened it on my phone while on the bus, and I almost missed my stop.

It wasn't a stranger writing in. It was someone walking through the same hallway as me. They didn't sign their name. They didn't have to.

I read it twice. Then I read it again. The second time, my chest got tight. I don't know what it is about reading something someone wrote in their own voice. It's not like a news story. It's like a person.

I wrote back in my head before I even got home. I was already a host, and we hadn't even recorded yet.

Dear Real Talk Podcast,

Me and Kayla have been best friends since fifth grade. We used to walk to school together, share everything, and I honestly thought we'd be close forever. But then she joined the volleyball team this year and everything changed.

Now she only hangs out with her teammates. She leaves me on read for days—I'm talking three or four days sometimes—and when I see her in the hallway, she barely even looks at me. It's like I'm invisible.

I don't want to come off clingy because I know she has a whole new thing going on. But I miss her, and I don't understand what I did wrong. We never even had a fight.

Is it okay to tell her I feel left behind, or will that just push her further away? How do I set a boundary without losing a friend?

—Invisible in the Hallway

Peer Responses from Middle & High School Students:

Hi Invisible. First, I have to tell you, I read your letter twice because the first time my eyes got watery. I feel you. I really do. Kayla joining volleyball isn't the problem. The problem is she stopped checking in. Those are two different things. You are not clingy for missing your friend. Try saying something simple, like: "Hey, I miss you. Can we plan one thing, just us, this month?" If she still acts like you're invisible after that, that tells you something. And it is not about who YOU are. You are not a locker. You are not the hallway. You are the whole entire hallway's favorite person, somewhere. Keep going.

—Real Talk Crew

I resonate deeply with the reality of a brewing separation. With that being said, the friendship and the closeness is not over as it is simply just waning. Your friend Kayla is not leaving you. Sometimes certain people just fade due to differing journeys. The two of you are starting to develop into different people for this time due to the different situations going on. Just as you may believe that it's looking bad, she may see it the exact same. A drift hurts both ends, but it's up to both of you to put in the effort to repair them. Ultimately, I believe that you should take a step back and allow her to ease back into the relationship if she wants to. If you don't think that helps, then have a talk about it to really understand why there is this strong hole in your relationship. From there, a fix is possible.

—Jalil, Teen Mental Health Ambassador (Newark, NJ)

Dear Invisible in the Hallway,

That sounds really hard. Going from being super close with someone to barely being acknowledged hurts especially when you don't even know what changed. Anyone in your position would feel confused and left out.

It doesn't sound like you did anything wrong. Sometimes people get caught up in new activities or friend groups and don't realize how their behavior is affecting others. That doesn't make it okay that she's ignoring you though.

It's okay to say something to her as long as you keep it simple and honest. Maybe something like, "Hey, I feel like we haven't talked much lately and I kind of miss hanging out." You're not accusing her; you're just telling the truth about how you feel. If she cares about the friendship, she'll at least try to meet you halfway, and she would understand how much that hurt you.

At the same time, don't feel like you have to keep chasing her if she keeps brushing you off. You deserve friends who actually notice you and want to spend time with you. It might not feel like it right now, but there are people out there who would appreciate you the way you deserve.

It's okay to miss her and still start opening yourself up to other friendships too. You don't have to replace her; you're just making space for people who show up for you.

You're not invisible, even if it feels that way right now.

—Emerline, Teen Mental Health Ambassador (Newark, NJ)

Dear invisible in the hallway,

I understand how you are feeling, and speaking from experience it is not fun feeling that way. But let me tell you something: you aren't a clingy friend so do not overthink it. Kayla just needs to become a better friend to you. Also, you should communicate your feelings to Kayla so that she understands what you're feeling, and if she doesn't want to understand, you should join a club and make new friendships. It may be hard, but you got this queen!

—Josephine, Teen Mental Health Ambassador (Newark, NJ)

Dear "Invisible in the Hallway,"

First, I just want to say—you're not invisible.

The way you care about your friendship and notice these changes shows how real and meaningful your connection with Kayla is.

It honestly sounds really painful to feel left behind like that, especially when nothing "bad" even happened. Friendships can change when people try new things, like joining a team, but that doesn't make your feelings any less important. You didn't do anything wrong. 🩶

It's okay to miss her. It's okay to feel hurt. And it's definitely okay to tell her how you feel.

You don't have to come off as clingy to be honest. You could say something simple like, "Hey, I miss hanging out with you. I know you've been busy, but I feel a little left out sometimes."

(That's not blaming her. It's just telling the truth.)

Also, remember this: one person growing in a different direction doesn't mean you stop mattering. It might just mean your life is making space for new people and friendships too.

You deserve friends who notice you, talk to you, and make you feel seen.

No matter what happens with Kayla, you won't stay invisible. Someone will see you—and choose you—fully. 🤍

—Lyric, Teen Mental Health Ambassador (Newark, NJ)

Grover Cleveland Student Response by Maki Beck

Dear Invisible in the Hallway,

You can be a better friend by telling Kayla how you feel. You can say, "I feel like you're leaving me," and give her a chance to understand what is hurting you.

Maki Beck drew a friend saying, "I feel like you're leaving me," and the other friend answering, "OK, I'm sorry."

Grover Cleveland Student Response by Zylon Bennett

Dear Invisible in the Hallway,

You can tell her how you feel. If she says yes and wants to talk, then maybe you've got your friend back. If she does not, you still told the truth.

Zylon Bennett drew two friends saying, "I miss you" and "I miss you too."

South 17th St. Student Response by Navaeh Robinson

Hey Invisible in the Hallway,

It seems like your friendship is changing, and that is okay. A big friendship can hurt when you have to let go, especially when you used to spend a lot of time together.

If you want closure, you could try to talk to Kayla one last time. But your mental health matters too. If the friendship is not good for you anymore, it is okay to find a person who does make you feel seen.

Real Talk Takeaway

A boundary is a line you draw to keep YOU safe. It can be as small as: "I need you to text me back this week."

You can miss someone and still be allowed to ask for what you need.

Chapter 2 Reflection Questions

1) Justin says he talks; he just doesn't love hearing his own voice played back. Is there a version of yourself that feels different *"from the inside"* than how others see you *"on the outside"*? Why do you think these two versions exist?

2) Justin's big motivation is his mom and his brother Marcus. Who or what motivates you when something feels hard or scary?

3) Justin's condition for joining was *"I get to say what I think."* What conditions, if any, would you set before joining something new like a group, a project, or a relationship?

4) **Your Turn:** Think of one person in your life whose sacrifice you rarely say anything about. Write one sentence acknowledging what they do. You don't have to send it to them (unless you want to).

Chapter 3

Mariposa Mic

narrated by Olivia

My friends, this is Olivia. The cover art was my job, obvio. Obvio means obvious in Spanish. Sometimes the Spanish word just shows up before the English one, and I let it.

I drew a microphone with butterfly wings. I drew it three times before I liked it. The first one had wings that looked like scary moths. The second one had a mouth, which was strange. The third one was perfect. Light, soft, like a tiny hopeful thing.

When I came to this city in fifth grade, I barely spoke English. People say it like it's a small thing. It is not a small thing. I was scared every day. I didn't understand jokes. Some kids laughed at the way I said certain words. I learned slang from a girl named Mia. She sat with me at lunch like it was the most normal thing in the world.

I think about Mia a lot. She is the reason I know what a real friend looks like. She is the reason I said yes to *Real Talk Podcast*.

Because Mia showed me: when you are new and scared, one person sitting next to you changes the whole school.

Dear Real Talk Podcast,

I used to be part of a group of four friends. We did everything together: lunch, weekends, everything. But lately I feel like a ghost that nobody can see anymore.

They have a group chat I'm not in. I know because they'll all laugh at something on their phones at the same time and nobody shows me. They make plans in front of me without inviting me, and when I walk up, they get quiet or change the subject.

I keep trying to be nice. I compliment them, I show up, I act like nothing's wrong. But it doesn't seem to matter.

How do I know when to keep trying to fix a friendship and when to let it go?

—*The Ghost at the Lunch Table*

Peer Responses from Middle & High School Students:

Hey Ghost. Don't take this the wrong way, but you are not a ghost. You are a whole person sitting next to people who are acting like they can't see you. That is on them, not you. I think the answer is: you keep trying until it costs you yourself. If trying is making you feel small, that is the line. Try one honest sentence with one of them: "Hey, can I ask if something happened? I've felt out of the group lately." If they say no, you'll learn something. If they say nothing, you'll also learn something. Either way you get an answer that isn't in your head anymore.

—Real Talk Crew

Grover Cleveland Student Response by Samuel Sawacha

Dear Ghost at the Lunch Table,

What I truly believe you should do is communicate your feelings and put yourself near the people you feel most comfortable with, instead of trying to fit in with a group that makes you feel invisible.

Grover Cleveland Student Response by Jahsyn Davis

Dear Ghost at the Lunch Table,

Try doing things together with people who treat you better. A real friend should include you, teach you things, learn from you, and make you feel like you belong.

Character drawing by Jahsyn Davis.

South 17th St. Student Response by Tatiyana Blue-Owens

Hi Ghost,

My advice to you is that maybe you are better off without friends who make you feel bad. I know it can hurt when people ignore you.

Try to build a better mindset when things get tough. Tell yourself how great you are, even if the people at the lunch table don't see it. Stay strong and get right.

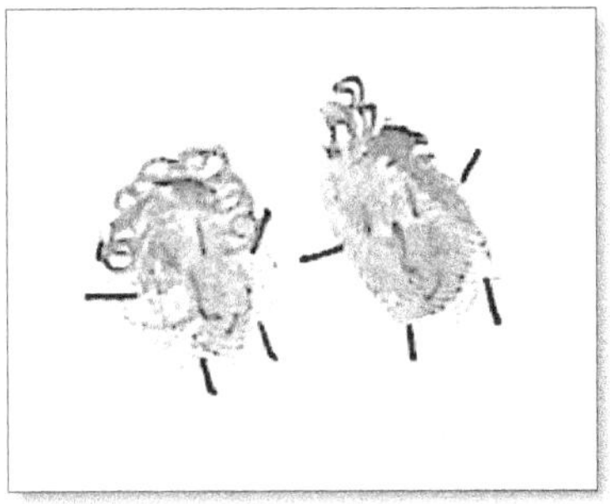

Doodle by Tatiyana Blue-Owens.

South 17th St. Student Response by Assiya Ameziane

Ghost, don't try to fix something that you haven't done wrong. I had the same situation too, so if they keep ignoring you, just let it go. It is not the end of the world.

Go make new friends who really listen, care, and invite you, even if you do not want to go at first. P.S. Don't push yourself past your limit. Be yourself.

Assiya drew a before-and-after friendship image with a "true friendship" heart.

Try This Sometime This Week

Draw your lunch table. Put yourself in the middle. Draw arrows showing who actually sees you. You don't have to show this drawing to anyone. Just notice.

Tee said we should record one whole episode before submitting anything to the contest. Justin said we should do two, because the first one was going to be bad. I said three, because patterns of three are how the universe works. Justin rolled his eyes at me. I drew a butterfly on his hand while he wasn't looking.

In my head I called it: *Real Talk Podcast, Episode 1. Real letters. Real us.*

Chapter 3 Reflection Questions

1) Olivia says learning a new language *"is not a small thing."* Have you ever felt like a fish out of water somewhere (for example: a new school, a new group, a new situation)? What made it harder or easier?

2) Olivia credits Mia for showing her *"what a real friend looks like."* Describe a time someone showed up for you in a way you didn't expect. What did they do?

3) *The Ghost at the Lunch Table* letter is about being quietly pushed out of a friend group. What do you think is the difference between drifting apart naturally and being deliberately excluded?

4) **Your Turn:** Think of someone in your life or school who might feel invisible right now. What is one small, specific thing you could do this week to make them feel seen?

Chapter 4

Day One in the Closet Studio

narrated by Tee

Our studio was a closet. Not a metaphor. A literal closet. Mr. Quintero teaches social studies, and he let us use the supply closet behind his room during lunch as long as we didn't knock anything over.

It smelled like old printer paper and cleaning spray. There was one folding chair. There was one borrowed microphone with a foam cover that looked like a tiny black cloud. There were three of us and one chair, so two of us sat on stacks of textbooks. That was the first sign that this would be a humbling experience.

Justin tested the mic. "Real Talk Podcast, episode one, take one." His voice came back like he was inside a metal pipe.

Olivia laughed so hard the mic had to be moved. She apologized in three languages.

I had a clipboard. Obviously. I had us set up to read three letters per episode and respond in two segments each. I had a timer. I had a checklist. Justin looked at the clipboard like it was a person who owed him money.

– group chat: REAL TALK CREW –

Justin: tee i love u but the clipboard is a lot

Tee: the clipboard stays.

Olivia: the clipboard is part of the show now

We started with a letter that scared me a little. It was about feeling locked in at home. Not a bad parent, the writer said. Just a parent who said no to everything. I wanted to handle it gently. I knew what it felt like to want freedom and to also love your family.

> *Dear Real Talk Podcast,*
>
> *I feel like my whole social life is controlled by my parent, and I don't know what to do about it. Every text I send gets read. Every time someone asks me to hang out, I have to ask permission. And the answer is almost always no.*
>
> *I know my parent isn't bad. They say it's for my protection, and I get that they care. But I'm suffocating. I have no real friendships because I can never actually go anywhere with anyone.*
>
> *Kids at school think I'm antisocial or just don't want to hang out. The truth is I'm not allowed. And when I try to talk about it at home, I get told I don't understand how the world works. Why do people feel the need to control others, even when they love them? How am I supposed to build real friendships when I can barely leave the house?*
>
> ***—Locked In on Maple Street***

Peer Responses from Middle & High School Students:

Locked In, can I say something? Your parent is scared. Their fear is a real feeling, and you don't have to fix it. You can love them and still ask for breathing room. Maybe start small: pick one thing you really want (one friend hangout, one club after school) and write down WHY it matters to you. Not in an arguing way. In a "here is who I want to be" way. Bring it to your parent like a project, not a fight. If you can, ask a trusted adult outside the house (a teacher, counselor, aunt, coach) to help you say it out loud. You are not antisocial. You are paying attention to how you feel and communicating it to your parent in a respectful way (which is not always easy). We're rooting for you!

—Real Talk Crew

Grover Cleveland Student Response by Samuel Sawacha

Dear Locked In on Maple Street,

What I truly believe you should do is communicate your feelings to your parent. Try to explain what you need and why it matters and ask for one small chance to show that you can handle more trust.

Samuel Sawacha drew a student saying, "Hey Dad, I want to express how I feel," and the dad answering, "OK, son."

Grover Cleveland Student Response by Jaden Loyal

Dear Locked In on Maple Street,

Let me go. I do not have to stay controlled by fear.

Illustration by Jaden Loyal about wanting freedom from fear.

South 17th St. Student Response by Mariyah Williams

Hey Locked In, I understand how you are feeling. I think you should tell your parents the truth about how their actions are making you feel. It is okay to feel embarrassed sometimes, but you should not have to feel alone.

Parents may act like that because they want you to stay safe. They may not want your phone or peers to brainwash you, and if they love you, taking your phone or saying "no" may be their way of trying to help you, not control you.

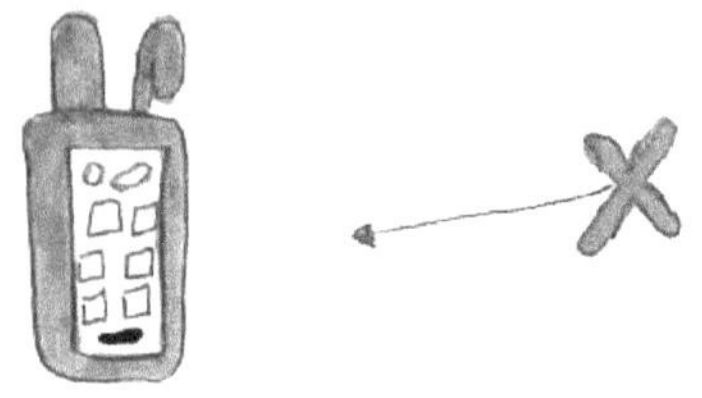

Mariyah created a phone-safety sketch, depicting how limited phone use could help protect us sometimes.

South 17th St. Student Response by Christina Jeudy

Dear Locked In, I think you should talk to your parents and explain how the rules make you feel. It can help to ask for one small thing first, like more trust or a little space, instead of trying to change everything all at once.

Parents may be scared, but young people still need respect and a chance to show responsibility.

Illustration by Christina.

🎙 Real Talk Takeaway

When the word "controlling" shows up in a relationship (even one made of love), it's worth saying out loud. Asking for space and still loving someone are not opposites.

Chapter 7

It Goes Viral (Kind Of)

🎙 *narrated by Tee*

I don't know exactly when Episode 3 "went viral." I just know that by Wednesday lunch, three sixth graders walked up to our table and said in unison, "you're Real Talk Podcast!"

It was like a movie scene. Olivia waved like a queen. Justin pulled his hoodie tighter. I almost knocked my milk over.

By Friday it had moved up into eighth grade. People I never talked to were quoting lines from the show in the hallway. Someone yelled "THE CLIPBOARD STAYS" at me at the water fountain. I tried not to smile. I smiled.

But then came the other side. The side I did not see coming.

Kids started trying to guess who wrote the letters. Out loud. In the cafeteria. "That ghost at the lunch table one—it's gotta be Mariah, right? Look how she sits." And worst of all: kids started fake-writing letters as a joke, hoping we'd read theirs and roast someone they didn't like.

📱 *— group chat: REAL TALK CREW —*

Tee: we have a problem.

Tee: people are guessing who wrote the letters

Justin: i KNEW this was gonna happen

Olivia: we need rules. like real ones. on the mic.

Tee: agenda for tomorrow lunch: privacy + respect rules

Justin: put it on the clipboard 😂

Chapter 4 Reflection Questions

1) The crew's "studio" was a literal closet with borrowed equipment. Have you ever had to make something work with almost nothing? What did you learn from that?

2) The *Locked In on Maple Street* letter describes a parent's love feeling like a cage. How do you think someone can care deeply about a person and still accidentally make them feel controlled?

3) One of the peer responses suggests bringing your need for freedom to a parent *"like a project, not a fight."* What do you think is the difference? Have you ever tried one approach vs. the other?

4) **Your Turn:** Think of one freedom you want that you haven't asked for yet. Write out the *"project version"* of that ask (the calm, clear, here's-why-it-matters version). It's OK if you choose not to use this version; just try writing it out.

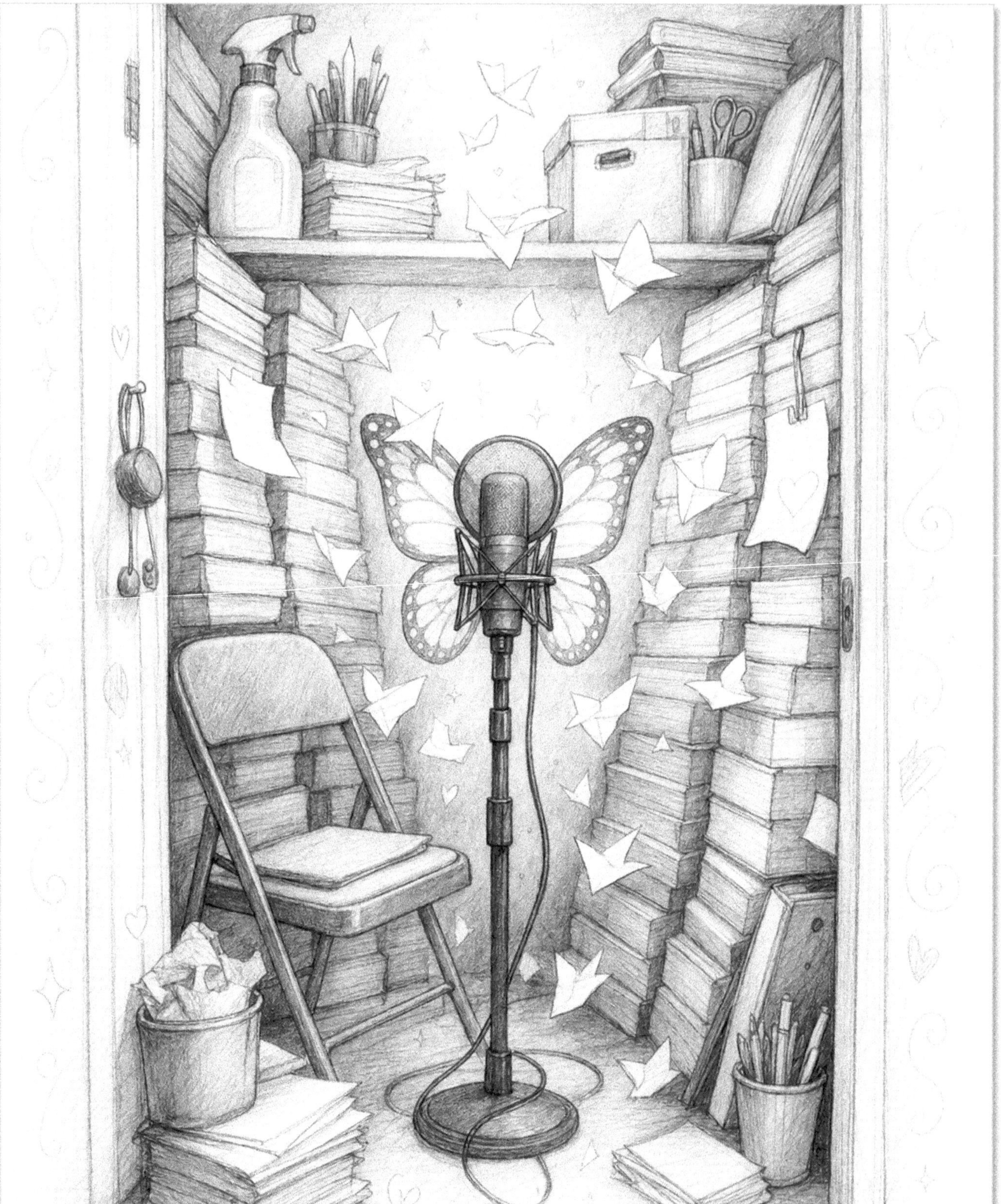

Chapter 5

Pressure

narrated by Justin

Episode two was the one where I almost lost it on the mic. I'm not proud. I'm also not unproud. Let me explain.

The letter was from someone calling themselves *Torn in Third Period.* They wrote about a person they liked who kept pressuring them to skip class and sneak out. The writer kept saying no. The other kid kept making them feel small for saying no.

Here is the thing. I know that kid. Not the writer. The OTHER one. Every school has one. The kid who says "you act like you're scared of everything" when really they just want company on the way down.

I read the letter on the mic and my jaw got tight. Olivia noticed. She put her hand on the table near mine. She didn't say anything. That was actually perfect.

> *Dear Real Talk Podcast,*
>
> *I like Marcus. I really do. But being with him is starting to stress me out more than anything else in my life right now.*
>
> *He keeps pressuring me to skip class with him and sneak out during lunch. When I say no, he acts like I'm being a baby. He'll say, "everyone does it" or "you act like you're scared of everything." And then he'll be cool and normal again and I forget about it—until the next time.*

I know getting in trouble would be a big deal for me. My mom would lose it. And honestly, I just don't want to do those things. But every time I say no I feel embarrassed, like maybe he's right and I'm being too much.

I don't want to lose him, but I also don't want to lose myself. What do I do when someone I like keeps pressuring me to do stuff that I'm not comfortable with?

—Torn in Third Period

Peer Responses from Middle & High School Students:

Real quick: you're not Marcus. You don't have to think like him or do the things he does, even if you all are dating. Saying no to something you don't want to do is not being a baby. It's being a person with your own mind. When somebody who likes you says, "you're scared of everything," that is not love talking. That is pressure dressed up like a joke. You don't have to break up with anyone today. But you do have to notice the pattern. Try saying out loud one time: "I'm not doing that. If you keep asking, I'm going to walk away from this conversation." See what happens. Watch how he acts. His next move is your answer.

—Real Talk Crew

Grover Cleveland Student Response by Nevaeh Lucas Wynn

Dear Torn in Third Period,

Hey, I see that you like Marcus, but have you talked to him about making you do things you don't want to do? You and Marcus should talk about the things you are not comfortable with, so he understands that you do not want to do them.

It is important to set boundaries with him. If he is making you sneak out during lunch and pressuring you, tell him that it is not okay and that you do not like it. If you keep allowing him to do things like that, he may think that it is okay.

No means no. Stop pushing me.

Grover Cleveland Student Response by Anaiyah Pressley

Dear Torn in Third Period,

No, thank you. I do not have to accept pressure that hurts me. Even if someone says, "It's just a joke," I can still say no and choose what feels respectful to me.

Illustrated response by Anaiyah Pressley about saying no to hurtful pressure.

South 17th St. Student Response by Skyy Leonard

Dear Torn in Third Period,

Have you considered breaking up with Marcus? I know it is hard to break up with someone, but if you are not really sure he is right for you (like he's controlling or trying to get you do the wrong things), it is okay to be honest. If you decide to break up, my advice is to do it in a safe way (maybe over the phone so there's some distance).

Do not pretend like things are fine just because you are scared to make things awkward. If he is pressuring you, that is not safe. You can break up if that is what you need to do.

Real Talk Takeaway

Pressure can wear the costume of a joke. The joke is not the issue. The pressure is the issue. You can like someone and still walk away from a bad idea.

After we wrapped, Olivia drew a tiny stop sign on the corner of my notebook. She wrote inside it: "I'm allowed." I keep that page taped to the inside of my locker now.

Chapter 5 Reflection Questions

1) Justin's jaw gets tight reading about pressure disguised as a joke. Why do you think pressure is harder to name when it comes from someone you actually like?

2) The *Torn in Third Period* letter describes someone who says *"you're scared of everything"* as a way to get their partner to go along. What does that phrase really communicate?

3) The Real Talk Takeaway says: *"Pressure can wear the costume of a joke."* Can you think of other *"costumes"* pressure sometimes wears? For example, are there other peer pressure phrases or behaviors that look like something else?

4) **Your Turn:** Practice saying this sentence out loud, alone: *"I'm not doing that."* Notice how it feels. Does it feel different depending on who you imagine saying it to?

Chapter 6

When "I Care" Means Something Else

narrated by Olivia

Today's letter was the hardest one we had read so far. We almost did not record it. We almost moved it to next week. But Tee said no; the people who need this letter the most are the people we'll reach through the harder episodes.

It was about jealousy. But not regular jealousy. The kind of jealousy that turns into checking phones and accusations and tears. The kind where someone says, "I do this because I care so much."

I have a tía (that means aunt) who lived through that. She is okay now. She is more than okay. She lives near the beach in Florida and sends me painted seashells. But it took her ten years to leave. Ten. Years.

When the writer used the words "he just gets scared," my hands got a little cold. Tee and Justin felt it too. I could see it on Tee's face.

> *Dear Real Talk Podcast,*
>
> *My partner Jordan asks to see my phone almost every day. Not in a playful way—like actually demands to scroll through it. If I hesitate even a little, Jordan gets upset and accuses me of hiding something or lying.*
>
> *Jordan also gets mad if I talk to other people for too long, even just classmates during a group project. I got accused of flirting once when I literally just asked someone for a pencil. And whenever I bring it up, Jordan says, "I do this because I care about you so much. I just get scared."*

My friends say it's controlling, and I should end it. But part of me feels bad because what if Jordan is just really insecure and needs reassurance? Like maybe this is what it looks like when someone really cares?

How do I know the difference between jealousy and actual control?

—Second-Guessing in Sixth Period

Peer Responses from Middle & High School Students:

Okay friend, I want to say this gently and also clearly. Care does not need access to your phone. Care does not get mad at you for asking for a pencil. When someone says "I'm doing this because I'm scared," what they are really saying is, "I want you to take care of my fear by giving up your freedom." That is an unfair trade. It costs you. Real love feels safe even when it feels new. If you are second-guessing yourself this much, that itself is information. Talk to a trusted adult about this, like a counselor, an aunt, anyone you trust. You are not making it up. You are noticing that something feels off.

—Real Talk Crew

Grover Cleveland Student Response by Chemean Lang

Dear Second-Guessing in Sixth Period,

This drawing shows how control can make a heart feel broken, watched, and trapped. If someone says they care about you but makes you feel like you cannot breathe, that is not the kind of love you deserve.

Student illustration about a broken heart held together by chains while eyes watch from around it.

South 17th St. Student Response by Stephanie Kromah

Dear Second-Guessing, I drew this to remind you that you can walk away.

South 17th St. Student Response by Angie Bowman

Dear Second-Guessing, if you do not feel safe talking about it, you should make a safety plan and ask a trusted adult who can protect you.

Never listen to a toxic person who makes you feel like you cannot make your own decisions. If someone is trying to control you, please talk to someone who can help you stay safe.

South 17th St. Student Response by Angeleah Darden

Dear Second-Guessing, if you do not feel safe talking about it, you should make a safety plan and ask a trusted adult who can protect you.

Never listen to a toxic person who makes you feel like you cannot make your own decisions. If someone is trying to control you, please talk to someone who can help you stay safe.

🎙 **Real Talk Takeaway**

Caring about someone never requires that you become smaller. If a relationship needs you to keep proving yourself, that is a red flag, not a love letter.

💡 **Try This Sometime This Week**

Write down three things that feel like CARE to you, and three things that feel like CONTROL. Notice if your list is one-sided.

Chapter 6 Reflection Questions

1) One of the peer responses says: *"Care does not need access to your phone."* Do you agree? Where do you think the line is between care and control?

2) Olivia shares that her aunt took ten years to leave a controlling relationship. Why do you think it can be so hard to leave a situation you know isn't good for you?

3) The writer of *Second-Guessing in Sixth Period* letter asks: *"What if Jordan is just really insecure and needs reassurance?"* How do you think compassion for someone's insecurity can sometimes be used against you?

4) **Your Turn:** Make two lists: three things that feel like *care* to you, and three things that feel like *control*. Notice whether any items could appear on both lists depending on the situation.

We sat in the closet studio with a granola bar each. Mr. Quintero pretended not to listen from his desk through the door. He listened.

We wrote the rules together. Then we read them on the next episode like the most serious people in the world.

Real Talk Privacy + Respect Rules (read on Episode 4)

1. We never guess. If you hear a letter that sounds like someone you know, you do not say their name. You do not even hint.
2. We never share. Letters do not leave this show. We do not screenshot. We do not forward.
3. We never fake. If a letter sounds like a prank to roast someone, we delete it without reading.
4. We tell an adult. If a letter sounds like someone is in danger, we tell a trusted adult right away.
5. We sign the same way: anonymous, on purpose. Names belong to the people who own them.

🎙 **Real Talk Takeaway**

When more people start listening, the stakes go up. That is when rules matter most.

Privacy is a kind of love. So is silence at the right time.

Chapter 7 Reflection Questions

1) When the podcast got popular, people started guessing who wrote the letters. Why do you think people get curious about other people's private pain? Why is acting on that curiosity harmful?

2) The Real Talk crew wrote five privacy rules together. Which rule do you think is the most important, and why?

3) Rule 4 says: *"If a letter sounds like someone is in danger, we tell a trusted adult right away."* Why is telling an adult in those cases not the same as breaking someone's trust?

4) **Your Turn:** Think about a time you shared something in confidence, and it spread further than you wanted—or a time you heard something private and felt the urge to pass it on. What would the Real Talk Privacy Rules have changed about that situation?

Chapter 8

The Joke and the Punchline

narrated by Justin

I want to talk about laughing. The kind that costs you something.

We got two letters in one week that hit me hard. One was from a kid called Laughing on the Outside. The other was The Punchline at Home. They were different, but they kind of held hands.

See, I'm the funny one. I know it. Tee is the planner, Olivia is the artist, I'm the jokester. I am good at making people laugh on the bus. I am good at making my brother laugh when we're eating cereal for dinner because Mom is pulling a double.

But there is a difference between making people laugh and making people the joke. I learned that on the mic.

Dear Real Talk Podcast,

My friend Devon has a way of making me the joke of every conversation. It's my clothes, my hair, the way I pronounce certain words. Devon will pick something and go in on it in front of whoever is around. And everyone laughs, so I laugh too. I act like it's funny.

But it's not funny. Every single time, it hurts. And when I've shown even a little bit that it bothered me, Devon immediately says, "I'm just playing, why are you so sensitive?" And then I feel stupid for being upset on top of already feeling embarrassed.

I don't want to make it a whole dramatic thing or cause problems in the whole friend group. Devon is still someone I hang out with every day, and I don't want things to be weird.

How do you tell someone they're hurting your feelings without it turning into a huge fight?

—Laughing on the Outside

Peer Responses from Middle & High School Students:

Laughing, you are not too sensitive. You are accurate. There is a difference. A real friend says sorry the first time. A real friend doesn't make a habit of putting you down in front of people just to see you flinch. Try pulling Devon aside (not in front of everyone) and saying something short and calm: "I know you call it playing, but it hurts. I need you to stop with the comments about my clothes and the way I talk." See what Devon does next. That's your answer. If they keep going, you have learned something important about who Devon is.

—Real Talk Crew

Dear Laughing on the Outside,

I'm really sorry you're dealing with this. What you're feeling is completely valid. Being laughed at or commented on like that, especially in front of others, is hurtful. Even if someone calls it a "joke," it does not make it okay if it is affecting you this much.

You deserve to feel comfortable and safe around your friends. It might help to talk to Devon privately, not in front of the group. You could say something simple like, "Hey, I know you might not mean it, but the comments about my clothes, my hair, and the way I talk actually bother me. Can you stop?" A real friend should respect that. If they do not, that says more about them than it does about you.

—Azyiah, Teen Mental Health Ambassador (Newark, NJ)

Grover Cleveland Student Response by Chuessy Saintime

Dear Laughing on the Outside,

If you truly feel bothered by Devon's jokes, you should try to respectfully and kindly communicate how you feel about them. Communicating how you feel is very important, because Devon may assume you're okay with those jokes since you have not yet shared your feelings.

Even though you value your friendship, I understand that feeling of wanting to express your feelings without ruining it. It's important that everyone in a friendship feels respected and comfortable. If you communicate with Devon and Devon is still not respectful of how you feel, you should probably step back from that friendship because it may be turning toxic.

Chuessy Saintime drew a student saying, "I do not like that."

> *Dear Real Talk Podcast,*
>
> *My older sibling Chris treats me like a joke. Not just at home—at family dinners, in front of my own friends, everywhere. The comments are always about something I care about: my music taste, my grades, the shows I watch. Chris calls me stupid like it's a nickname.*
>
> *When I say it bothers me, Chris laughs it off like I'm being dramatic. And my parents just say, "that's what siblings do, you two are so dramatic." So now I feel like I can't even complain about it without being dismissed.*
>
> *I'm tired of being the punchline. It's gotten to the point where I don't want to bring anyone over to my house because I don't want to be embarrassed in front of them.*
>
> *How do I get Chris to understand that none of this is actually funny? And how do I make it stop when the adults at home act like it's totally normal?*
>
> *—The Punchline at Home*

Peer Responses from Middle & High School Students:

Punchline. You are not dramatic. You are tired. There is a HUGE difference. When the people at home laugh too, it's easy to start believing maybe you are the problem. You are not. Try this: pick one trusted adult OUTSIDE the house. A coach, a teacher, an auntie, anyone. Tell them the same way you told us. Having one person on the outside who sees it clearly will help you. And next time Chris pulls a joke at your expense in front of someone, you're allowed to leave the room. You don't have to perform calm for a comedian who isn't funny.

—Real Talk Crew

Dear Punchline at Home,

First, I want to say that I admire your patience and love for your family. It is completely normal to need privacy and space, and that does not make you a bad sibling or a dramatic person. What you described, not being heard and feeling watched or laughed at, can be very stressful.

Setting boundaries is not about pushing people away. It is about making the relationship healthier so you can actually enjoy time together. When you talk to your family, try starting with love, stating the boundary, and ending with love. You can say, "I love you, but those comments hurt me, and I need them to stop." You can care about your family and still take care of yourself.

—Audrey, Teen Mental Health Ambassador (Newark, NJ)

Grover Cleveland Student Response by Joel Rivas

Dear Punchline at Home,

Your family says that Chris's nickname is funny, and he just laughs it off. But when you bring it up, they act like you're being dramatic. Your parents don't understand that it hurts. I think you should tell them all clearly: it may be funny to them, but it is not funny to you.

Grover Cleveland Student Response by Mai Lah Loyal-Murphy

Dear Punchline at Home,

I've been in your shoes before, where I felt like every time I asked for respect or talked about my feelings, I would end up getting guilt-tripped into apologizing. My best advice is to have a serious talk with your sibling. Prepare what you're going to say, sit them down in a quiet environment, and tell them how you feel.

Don't be too soft about it, because then they may walk all over you. Set your foot down and be a little stern. Let them know that what they are doing is wrong and that it hurts your feelings. Communication is key.

Then tell your parents how you feel and what's been going on. Tell them that you don't feel respected. If things continue, tell a trusted adult so you can get real-life advice. Good luck.

Real Talk Takeaway

"I'm just playing" is not an apology. It's a way to skip the apology. Some jokes are little knives in a soft voice. You are allowed to put the knives down or leave the kitchen.

Chapter 8 Reflection Questions

1) Justin says there is a difference between *making people laugh* and *making people the joke*. What is that difference, in your own words?

2) In the *Laughing on the Outside* letter, the writer laughs along even though it hurts. Have you ever laughed at something that actually stung? Why do we do that?

3) In *The Punchline at Home* letter, the parents dismiss the sibling behavior as *"that's just what siblings do."* How does it feel when adults minimize something that really hurts? What do you wish they would say instead?

4) **Your Turn:** Write down a joke someone has made at your expense that you never actually found funny. You don't have to show anyone. Just give yourself permission to call it what it is.

Chapter 9

Mia Energy

narrated by Olivia

This is the letter I had been waiting for. I didn't know it until I read it.

It came from someone called New Here but Not Alone. They moved to our city from another country less than a year ago. They were terrified every day at first. And then a girl named Mia sat down next to them at lunch like it was nothing.

My Mia. Not literally my Mia. But also, yes. My Mia. I read that letter in the closet studio, and I had to put my hand over my mouth so no one could hear me cry.

After we recorded, I asked Tee and Justin if we could call this energy something. Justin said "Mia Energy." I said yes. Tee said we needed to put it on a tote bag. Justin said no tote bags. We voted. We did not get tote bags. But the name stuck.

Dear Real Talk Podcast,

I moved to Newark from another country less than a year ago, and I barely spoke English when I started school here. I was terrified every single day. I didn't know how anything worked, I couldn't understand jokes, and some kids would laugh at the way I talked.

Then Mia started sitting with me at lunch. She didn't make it weird. She just sat down and started talking to me like it was normal. She helped me with homework, translated words for me, taught me slang, and one day when someone mocked my accent, she said something back to them. I didn't even ask her to.

Because of Mia, school doesn't feel impossible anymore. I never had a friend like that before, and I want to be that kind of person for someone else someday.

How do I be a good friend back to Mia? And how do I become the kind of friend who shows up for people the way she showed up for me?

—New Here but Not Alone

Peer Responses from Middle & High School Students:

Friend, first of all, gracias for being brave enough to write. (Gracias means thanks.) You don't have to do anything big to be a good friend back to Mia. Tell her, out loud, what you just told this podcast. People rarely hear how much they matter. Say it. Even one sentence: "You changed my school year. I wanted you to know." And being "a Mia" for someone else? You already are. The fact that you want to be—that IS the Mia energy. The next new kid? You'll see them. You'll sit down. You'll translate. You'll show them they're not alone.

—Real Talk Crew

Dear New Here but Not Alone,

Reading your letter brought back so many memories. I moved to Newark from Nigeria when I was in third grade, and those first few months felt exactly like what you are describing. I remember the fear of not knowing how things worked and the way some kids would look at me when I spoke. It is hard when you feel like you are on the outside looking in.

I am so happy you found your Mia. Having one person who sees you as a person and not just "the new kid" changes everything. You are already being a good friend by appreciating her. If you want to give back, share your world with her. Tell her about your culture and the things you love. True friendship is a two-way street where both people learn from each other.

You also have a superpower now, which is empathy. Because you know what it feels like to be mocked or confused, you may be the first to notice when a new student is sitting alone. You do not need a big speech. Just sit down, say hi, and treat them like it is normal. You are not just "the new kid" anymore. You are becoming a leader who knows how to build bridges.

—Fawaz, Teen Mental Health Ambassador (Newark, NJ)

Grover Cleveland Student Response by Jahsyn Davis

Dear New Here but Not Alone,

You should try teaching Mia your language too, like she helped teach you English and slang. You can also show her your culture, try to do things together, give each other small gifts if you want, and treat each other better. That is how both friends learn from each other.

Grover Cleveland Student Response by Taurisa Redding

Dear New Here but Not Alone,

Real friends stay.
You are kind.
I am here for you.
Smile.

Taurisa Redding's illustrated reminder:
"Real Friends Stay. You are Kind."

South 17th St. Student Drawing by Kamila Osario

Kamila's response focuses on being loyal, respectful, and helping a friend feel included.

Try This Sometime This Week

Find the newest kid in your grade. Just say hi this week. That is all. Don't make it a project. Just hi.

Bonus: at lunch, the empty seat next to a new kid is a magic chair. Sit in it.

Dear Real Talk Podcast,

My parents are going through a divorce and this year has been the hardest of my life. I've been angry, sad, and honestly pretty terrible to be around. I shut a lot of people out because I didn't want to explain anything or get pitied.

But my friend Elijah never stopped showing up. He walks with me after school even when I don't feel like talking. He'll just bring snacks and sit with me and not make it weird. When I finally did talk about what was going on, he just listened. No advice, no "everything happens for a reason." Just listened.

I don't think I've ever had a friend like that before. And now that I'm slowly feeling more like myself, I want to be that for someone else someday.

How do you become the kind of friend who knows when to show up and what to do when words aren't enough?

—Grateful in Room 112

Peer Responses from Middle & High School Students:

Grateful, Elijah sounds like the kind of friend most of us would draw if we could draw friends. Snacks. Silence. No fixing. That is so much harder than it looks. You are already learning how to be that friend, just by noticing that he did it. The kind of friend you're describing doesn't need a script. They just need a chair next to yours. Next time someone you love is going through something—don't bring advice, bring presence. A bag of chips and an open seat is more powerful than any quote you could send.

—Real Talk Crew

Grover Cleveland Student Response by Cherifa Tidjani

Dear Grateful in Room 112,

I'm so sorry to hear about your parents' divorce. I can relate, because I've been through something like that and it wasn't easy. I know how it feels, but the only difference was that I didn't have someone to be there for me. So the fact that you have someone there to comfort you is amazing. Those types of friends are the real ones.

My advice is to hold your head up and try to push through. Your friend Elijah is a true friend, someone who is going to be there through thick and thin. Be there for him like he was there for you. Understand each other and don't take him for granted. The bond that you have is incredible. Cherish what you have.

Cherifa Tidjani drew a heart about friendship being key to a strong bond.

South 17th St. Student Response by Alyssa Coleman

Dear Grateful in Room 112, there are many ways to be there for your friends. One thing for sure is that you can learn from your own mistakes. A lot of people do that and share their advice about how to fix their mistakes.

A second way is to learn from positive people. When you hang around positive people, they tend to give out a lot of good advice and can be a type of therapy person toward your friends, or that positive person can be someone you consider your mentor.

Dear Grateful in Room 112,

My parents went through a rough breakup too, so I get where you're coming from. It is hard seeing two people you love and care about not getting along. Like you, I was angry and confused. But I'm glad you noticed that shutting people out was not helping. That kind of honesty takes accountability.

Some people may not be trying to pity you. They may be trying to understand. There is a big difference between pity and empathy. Pity is when someone feels sorry for you. Empathy is when someone tries to understand what you are feeling and see things from your point of view.

You do not owe everybody an explanation about what you are going through. But you can still tell people what you need. You could say, "I'm dealing with something big right now, and I'm not ready to talk about it yet, but I still want you to be there for me." That is how healthy boundaries work. Boundaries do not shut people out. They help people understand how to care for you.

The real ones, like Elijah, will respect those boundaries. Elijah showed up without pressuring you. He walked with you, brought snacks, and let you be quiet when you needed to be quiet. Sometimes being a good friend means reading the room. Does your friend seem unusually upset? Is their voice quieter than usual? Are they less talkative? Those are clues that they may need support.

When someone is going through something, do not always rush to give advice. You can ask, "Do you want advice, or do you just need me to listen?" If they want advice, give it with care. If they just need to vent, listen and let them feel heard.

I'm happy you want to be the kind of friend Elijah was to you. That shows how kindness can spread. I wish you the best in your friendships and in your healing from your parents' divorce.

—Shyann, Teen Mental Health Ambassador (Newark, NJ)

🎙 **Real Talk Takeaway**

Some friendships are loud. The best ones are often quiet. Showing up is a love language. Even when nobody's asking for it.

Chapter 9 Reflection Questions

1) Olivia connects deeply with the *New Here but Not Alone* letter because it reminds her of what an old friend from elementary school did for her. Why do you think being welcomed can stay with someone for a long time?

2) The crew calls this kind of kindness *"Mia Energy."* What does Mia Energy mean to you? What actions show that someone has it?

3) Both letter writers want to know how to be a good friend back to the people who showed up for them. Why can it sometimes feel hard to thank someone for helping you, even when you are grateful?

5) **Your Turn:** Think of someone who made school, a group, or a hard season easier for you. Write one sentence you could say to let them know they mattered.

Chapter 10

Caught in the Middle

narrated by Tee

The contest deadline crept up on us. We had three weeks. We had to record one episode that was extra special, the "submission episode," the one the judges would actually listen to.

I had a list. Obviously. I had us picking the letters that showed range—friendship, family, romance, identity. The judges needed to feel that we could go from light to deep without tripping.

And then I got a text from Kayla. My Kayla. Old-Kayla. The one who left me on read for three days at a time.

It said: "Hey. I miss you. Can we talk?"

I stared at my phone like it was speaking French. I had to stop what I was doing. The text felt like a letter to our podcast.

– group chat: REAL TALK CREW –

Tee: kayla just texted me. she said she misses me.

Olivia: TEEEEE 😱😱

Justin: wait. how do you feel about that.

Tee: ...i don't know. is that bad?

Justin: nah. that's honest.

Olivia: go for a walk first. don't text back now.

Then we got a letter that felt like the universe was watching me. It was from Caught in the Middle. Someone whose best friend was acting jealous because they made new friends in drama club.

I read it three times. And I cried in the closet a little. Justin pretended he didn't see. Olivia hugged me from the side, no big deal, no scene.

> *Dear Real Talk Podcast,*
>
> *I joined drama club this year and made some new friends, which honestly has been one of the best things to happen to me. But now my best friend Jasmine is acting like I betrayed her.*
>
> *She gives me one-word answers when I text. She'll say things like "I guess you don't need me anymore" and then change the subject. One time I invited her to hang out with my drama friends, and she said, "I don't want to be someone's charity case." I wasn't treating her like that.*
>
> *I still care about Jasmine. She's been my best friend for years. But I also want to have other friends, and I don't think that should be a crime.*
>
> *Is it normal for a best friend to act jealous when you make new friends? How do I handle this without losing Jasmine or giving up my new friendships?*
>
> *—Caught in the Middle*

Peer Responses from Middle & High School Students:

Caught, I'm going to say something kind and also true. Jasmine's feelings are real, and also, they are not your job to fix by shrinking. Growing your circle is not betrayal. It is being alive. Try saying to her, gently and in person: "You're my best friend. I'm not replacing you. I'm allowed to have more than one good thing." If she keeps pulling away after that, that is a Jasmine problem, not a you problem. You can love someone and still let them figure out their own jealousy in their own time.

—Real Talk Crew

Dear Caught in the Middle,

It's normal for a best friend to feel jealous when you make new friends, but their behavior should not be hurtful or controlling. Jasmine's one-word answers, passive-aggressive comments, and refusal to meet your new friends are red flags. You value your friendship with her, but you also deserve to enjoy your new connections without feeling guilty.

Consider talking to her directly and honestly about your feelings. Use "I" statements to explain how her words and actions are impacting you, and reassure her that your new friendships do not erase your bond. Let her know you want to include her in your life, but you cannot control who you are friends with. Set gentle boundaries and prioritize your own happiness. If she continues to be negative or distant, you may need to reevaluate the friendship. True friends support each other's growth and happiness.

—Madisyn, Teen Mental Health Ambassador (Gary, IN)

Grover Cleveland Student Response by Quamel Green

Dear Caught in the Middle,

My advice is to have a one-on-one conversation with your best friend to give her a clearer picture of what's been happening. Express your feelings while also making an effort to understand hers. If she is a real friend, she will understand your reasoning behind your actions.

Quamel Green illustrated feeling pulled between two friend groups.

Grover Cleveland Student Response by Jonathan Jordan

Dear Real Talk Listeners,

It's okay to change. Everything changes. There's no need to worry about your friends making new ones. And if you do grow apart from old friends, that's okay too. Just remember the good times you had with them, and maybe see it as an opportunity to make new friends of your own.

South 17th Street Student Response by Fathiat Yussuff

Everyone has their own feelings and opinions, so it is okay for Jasmine to feel that way. But if she sees you with other people, she should still talk to you and express her feelings instead of making you feel bad.

No one should make you feel like you lost someone just because you made new friends. If she rejects you, maybe it is for the best. You can also continue to make new friends through a sport, hobby, or activity.

South 17th Street Student Response by Amy Mayorga Fierro

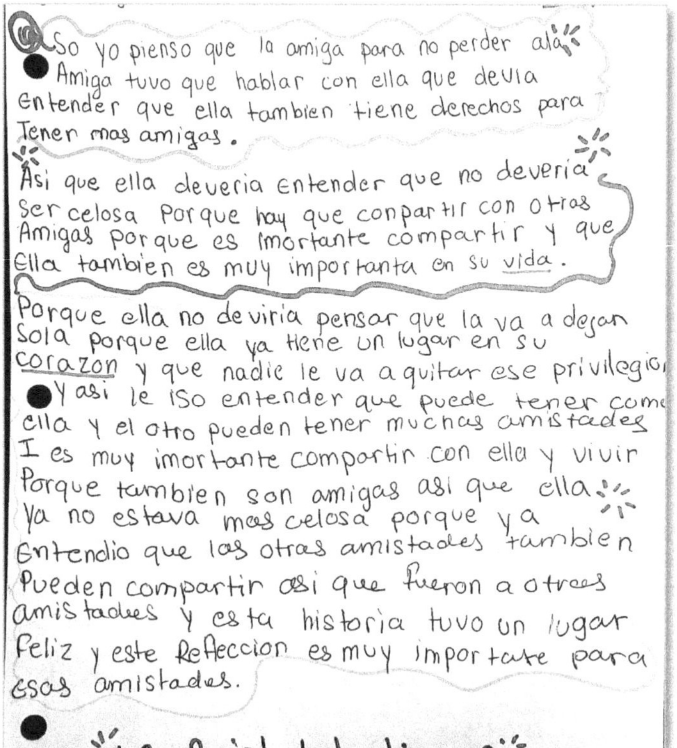

So yo pienso que la amiga para no perder ala
Amiga tuvo que hablar con ella que devia
entender que ella tambien tiene derechos para
Tener mas amigas.

Asi que ella deveria entender que no deveria
Ser celosa porque hay que conpartir con otras
Amigas porque es imortante compartir y que
Ella tambien es muy importanta en su vida.

Porque ella no deviria pensar que la va a dejar
Sola porque ella ya tiene un lugar en su
corazon y que nadie le va a quitar ese privilegio,
Y asi le iso entender que puede tener como
ella y el otro pueden tener muchas amistades
I es muy imortante compartir con ella y vivir
Porque tambien son amigas asi que ella
ya no estava mas celosa porque ya
Entendio que las otras amistades tambien
Pueden compartir asi que fueron a otras
amistades y esta historia tuvo un lugar
Feliz y este Refleccion es muy importate para
esas amistades.

LA Amistad tambien es
importante

Amy's response explains that a friend can still matter even when you have other friendships.

South 17th Street Student Response by Fathiat Yussuff

It is normal for your best friend to get jealous when you make new friends because they might feel like you are leaving them out.

But in a friendship, there should be care and respect. Talk to your friend, and maybe they will feel better once they understand you still care.

🎙 Real Talk Takeaway

New friends are not a betrayal of old friends. You can grow your circle without shrinking your past. You are allowed.

Then another letter came in that made the room get quiet. This one was not from the person being hurt by jealousy. It was from the person feeling jealous. I almost did not want to read it out loud, because it was honest in a way that made everybody sit up straighter.

Dear Real Talk Podcast,

I'm going to be honest. I'm writing about myself and not something someone else is doing to me. I'm the jealous one in my relationship, and I don't know how to stop.

Whenever Sam talks to someone else for more than a few minutes, I feel this panic in my chest. I check Sam's social media constantly, like multiple times an hour, looking for something. I pick fights over things that don't even make sense when I say them out loud. I know Sam hasn't done anything wrong. I know I'm being irrational. But I can't stop.

I don't want to be this person. I've already noticed Sam getting frustrated, and I'm scared I'm going to ruin something that actually matters to me. But I don't know where this feeling even comes from or how to deal with it without just blowing up.

How do I handle jealousy when I know the problem is me? Is there a way to work through this without ruining my relationship?

—The Jealous One

Peer Responses from Middle & High School Students:

Dear The Jealous One, first, we have to give you credit for telling the truth. A lot of people act jealous and then blame everybody else. You noticed it was happening inside of you, and that is a big first step.

But being honest does not mean you get to keep hurting Sam. Checking Sam's page all day, picking fights, and trying to control who Sam talks to is not healthy. That panic feeling may be real, but it is not proof that Sam did something wrong.

Try this: when the jealous feeling hits, pause before you text, post, accuse, or investigate. Ask yourself, "What am I afraid of right now?" Maybe you are scared of being left out, replaced, embarrassed, or not enough. That fear needs care, but it does not get to be the boss of your relationship.

You should also talk to Sam when you are calm, not in the middle of a fight. You could say, "I know I have been acting jealous. I am working on it. I do not want to make my fear your problem." And if the feeling keeps taking over, talk to a counselor, trusted adult, or therapist if you can. Jealousy is a feeling. Control is a choice. You can feel the feeling without choosing the control.

—Real Talk Crew

South 17th Street Student Response by Karizza Weaver

Dear The Jealous One,

I understand your problem and that you are worried about your partner talking to someone else. That can feel hard, but it is okay to talk about your feelings instead of holding them in or turning them into jealousy.

Maybe try talking to your partner about your jealousy issues when you are both calm. Even if you do not want to, sometimes the best thing to do is work on your own issues, take space when you need it, or find someone you trust who can give you reassurance and help you work through your feelings. I wish you the best in your relationship.

Grover Cleveland Student Response by Mason Barnett

I can change.

Get out, jealousy.

Share and trust yourself.

Mason Barnett drew jealousy as something you can face and push away.

Grover Cleveland Student Response by Kyle Santos Olivo

Kyle Santos Olivo created a "Just be Happy" poster response.

South17th St. Student Response by Damaris Quinatoa

Damaris created an illustration about overcoming jealousy

🎙 Real Talk Takeaway

Jealousy is a feeling, but it cannot be the driver. A healthy relationship gives people room to breathe, have friends, and be trusted. If jealousy shows up, the goal is not to pretend it is not there. The goal is to pause, tell the truth, and deal with the fear underneath it before it turns into control

I texted Kayla back that night. I said, “I miss you too. Can we walk after school Friday?” She said yes. We are not best friends like before. We are something new—slower, more honest. And that is okay. That is more than okay.

Chapter 10 Reflection Questions

1) Tee gets a text from Kayla and does not know how to feel. Why can it be confusing when someone who hurt you wants to come back into your life?

2) In *"Caught in the Middle,"* one friend feels jealous because another friend is making new friends. What is the difference between missing someone and trying to control them?

3) In *"The Jealous One,"* the writer admits that they are the problem. Why is it brave to admit when your own feelings are hurting a relationship?

4) The Real Talk Crew says, *"Jealousy is a feeling. Control is a choice."* What do you think that means?

5) **Your Turn:** Think of a time when you felt left out, jealous, or worried someone was replacing you. What is one healthy thing you could say or do instead of blaming, checking their social media pages, or starting a fight?

Chapter 11

The Walls Get Thinner

narrated by Justin

Episode 6 was almost not made. I want to say that first. We talked about postponing. We almost did.

Because the letters that week were the heavy ones. The ones where you read them and then you don't want to eat dinner. The ones where your hands feel cold even though it's warm in the closet studio.

Tee made the call. She said: "If we don't talk about this, we're telling kids the show isn't for them." She was right. She is usually right. Don't tell her I said that though.

But we did one new thing first. Olivia drew a little box at the bottom of every page in the script that read: "If this is your life, tell a trusted adult." We promised on the mic we would say it out loud. Every. Single. Letter.

> *Dear Real Talk Podcast,*
>
> *I love my partner Lena but being in this relationship is exhausting in a way I can't even fully explain. It's like I spend all my time worried about saying or doing the wrong thing. If I hang out with my friends, Lena gets hurt and says I don't make her a priority. If I take more than an hour to text back (even if I'm literally in class), Lena will send a string of messages and then say, "I guess I just don't matter to you." One time I used the wrong word in a sentence and Lena cried and said, "if you really loved me, you'd know what I need."*
>
> *I'm constantly apologizing for things I'm not even sure I did wrong. And then after, Lena is sweet, and things are fine, and I feel like maybe I was overthinking it. But then it happens again. How do I tell the difference between someone who is emotional and someone who is using emotions to control me?*
>
> ***—Walking on Eggshells***

Peer Responses from Middle & High School Students:

Eggshells. You are not crazy. You are tired. There is a name for what you're describing, and it has nothing to do with you being too much. When you are constantly afraid of saying the wrong thing, that is your body telling you the relationship is not safe. I don't mean unsafe in a movie way, but unsafe in a quiet, everyday way. Please talk to a trusted adult. A counselor at school. A parent. An aunt. Someone older who can hear the whole pattern and not just the moments where Lena is sweet again. You deserve to relax in your own life.

—Real Talk Crew

Grover Cleveland Student Response by Anssou Dore

Dear Walking on Eggshells,

A relationship seems unhealthy when someone keeps pushing the other person away or making them nervous. They need to be friendly and talk respectfully, not ignore you for days or make you feel bad. Sometimes people can be unhappy, but they also have to give time and respect to the people in their life.

Anssou Dore drew two friends trying to start over with kindness, respect, and love.

South 17th St. Student Response by Izaevonia House

Hi, Walking on Eggshells, I understand what you're going through because I've been there myself. You should tell Lena that you have your own life and that you love her, but she is being really controlling. That is not really a healthy relationship.

A relationship should not be so stressful that you feel like you do not have room to breathe. Try to communicate what you need and ask for help if she does not understand.

South 17th St. Student Response by Johanna Valenzuela

You can handle this situation by talking as a couple because that is needed in a relationship. Communication matters, and each person should try to understand the other person's problem.

If it is too hard to work through by yourself, look for help from someone experienced. A relationship is not only one person's feelings. It should be both people trying to understand each other.

Dear Real Talk Podcast,

This isn't about me; it's about my best friend, Naya. And I'm scared for her.

Naya's partner controls basically everything in her life right now. Who she talks to, what she wears, when she's allowed to be on her phone. If Naya does something her partner doesn't like, there's a huge reaction—yelling, guilt trips, sometimes ignoring her for days. I've watched this happen.

When I try to bring it up, Naya shuts me down. She says her partner is "just protective" and that I don't understand. The last time I said something, she got defensive and didn't talk to me for a week.

I'm scared that if I keep pushing, I'll lose her completely. But I'm also scared of what happens if I say nothing.

How do I tell a friend that their relationship seems unhealthy without pushing them away?

—Worried from the Sideline

Peer Responses from Middle & High School Students:

Hey Worried, first, you are already a good friend just by writing this. Two truths: you cannot make Naya leave a controlling relationship. AND you can be the safe place she comes back to. Both are real. Stop trying to convince her. Instead, say once, clearly: "I love you. I don't love how he/she/they treat you. I am here whenever you need me—no questions, no I-told-you-sos." Then keep being there. Don't disappear because she pushed you away once. People in controlling relationships often get isolated from their friends; your steady presence matters even when she seems mad. And please, talk to a trusted adult about Naya. A counselor, a teacher, a coach, a parent of hers if you trust them. This is not snitching. This is loving her louder than her fear.

—Real Talk Crew

South 17th St. Student Response by Toliya Lowe

Dear Worried from the Sideline, I think it would be best if you tell your best friend that her relationship is really mentally and emotionally draining. If she cannot see the problem, you still do not have to get dragged down and stressed about her choices. You can care about someone and still ask an adult for help when you are worried about their safety.

South 17th St. Student Response by Angeleah Darden

If the relationship does not give freedom, it may not be healthy. Naya should not feel trapped, and a friend can help by reminding her that her feelings matter.

South 17th St. Student Response by Ashley Coca

Hey Worried, I understand why you are worried and scared for her. You should set your own boundaries too, because you cannot force your friend to leave before she is ready. Comfort her and keep telling her you care.

If what is happening feels dangerous, talk to an adult who can help.

Ashley created an llustration with the message "Go through the rainbow to find true color" and "feel your emotions."

If a relationship feels unsafe

Tell a trusted adult right now—a parent, counselor, teacher, coach, librarian, faith leader, school nurse, or relative.

You can also reach the U.S. National Domestic Violence Hotline by phone or text. Search "national domestic violence hotline" for current numbers.

You do not have to be 100% sure something is wrong to ask for help.

🎙 Real Talk Takeaway

Walking on eggshells is not love. It is exhaustion in disguise. If a relationship feels unsafe or scary, tell a trusted adult. That is not drama. That is safety.

Dear Real Talk Podcast,

I think something might be wrong with me. Every friendship and relationship I get into ends up being dramatic or controlling or messy in some way—and the really messed up part is that I think I like it.

When things are calm and stable, I get bored. Like I actually feel bored. Normal friendships where people are just nice to each other feel flat to me, almost fake. But then when there's tension and jealousy and on-again-off-again situations, I feel more alive.

I've noticed the pattern. I keep choosing people who are controlling, or who make me feel like I have to work for their attention. Even when I know it's not good for me, I stay. Or I leave and find someone exactly the same.

Is it possible to want something that's hurting you? Will I ever be able to be happy in a healthy relationship?

—Addicted to the Drama

Peer Responses from Middle & High School Students:

Real talk, Drama—yes. It is possible to want something that hurts you. It's actually really common. We sometimes get used to a feeling and call that feeling "love." Calm can feel boring when chaos is what you trained on. That is not a flaw in you. It is just a pattern. Patterns can be unlearned, slowly. Please ask a trusted adult or counselor about therapy or talk groups in your area. This is the kind of stuff that gets easier with someone trained to listen. And in the meantime, when calm shows up, sit with it. Don't poke it to make sure it's real. Just let it be quiet. You can do this.

—Real Talk Crew

South 17th St. Student Response by Naziyah Green

Dear Addicted to the Drama, I know you like the toxic-ness, but how are you going to be free in life if you have no friends because you like being toxic?

There will be a time in life when you need a friend. Try to think about whether the drama is really helping you or just keeping you stuck.

South 17th St. Student Response by Zyneira Weaver

Hey there, I know you like drama, but sometimes it is not good. People can keep making drama because they are used to it, but that can lead people to have no friends.

If you want something that hurts you, that is a sign that you may need help breaking the habit. If you want a healthy relationship, try to get out of the habit of being around drama.

> 🎙 **Real Talk Takeaway**
>
> Drama can feel exciting when calm is not what you are used to. But familiar does not always mean healthy. You can notice the pattern, ask for help, and practice letting peace feel normal.

Chapter 11 Reflection Questions

1) Justin says some letters are so heavy they make your hands feel cold. Why is it important to talk about serious topics carefully instead of pretending they do not exist?

2) In the Walking on Eggshells and Worried from the Sideline letters, people are scared because a relationship feels controlling. What are some signs that a relationship may not be safe or healthy?

3) Worried from the Sideline wants to help Naya but does not want to push her away. What could a friend say or do to show love without making the person feel judged?

4) **Your Turn:** Addicted to the Drama says calm relationships can feel boring or fake at first. Write down one sign of a healthy relationship that you want to practice trusting, even if it feels new.

Chapter 12

When It Feels Okay, You Still Have to Believe It

narrated by Justin

Episode 8 was the one nobody saw coming. The letter was nice. Like genuinely, calmly nice. The writer wasn't in trouble. They were just... confused that things were good.

Their partner Aiden listened to them. Said "okay" when they said no. Asked how they were feeling and waited for the answer. The writer kept waiting for the catch.

I get that. I get it so much. When you grow up watching certain kinds of arguing, calm feels suspicious. Like, "okay, when does this turn?" You start to think the storm IS the relationship, and the calm is just the trick.

> *Dear Real Talk Podcast,*
>
> *I know this might sound weird but I'm writing because I don't actually have a problem. I just don't know if what I have is real.*
>
> *I just started dating Aiden, and it's honestly kind of confusing me because it's so different from what I've seen. When I say I'm not comfortable with something, Aiden just says "okay, no problem"—no attitude, no guilt trip, nothing. Aiden actually asks me how I'm feeling and then listens to the answer. Like actually listens.*
>
> *I keep waiting for the catch. In every relationship I've seen—with friends, with family, with*

people at school—someone always ends up getting controlled or talked down to. So when things feel this easy and calm, I start wondering if something's wrong with me for not trusting it.

Is this really what a healthy relationship is supposed to feel like? How do I stop waiting for things to go bad?

—Surprised in a Good Way

Peer Responses from Middle & High School Students:

Yes. This is what it is supposed to feel like. Boring, in the best way. Quiet, in the best way. If your brain keeps waiting for the "real" version of Aiden to show up—that is not Aiden. That is your old experience trying to protect you. Thank it, then tell it you are safe here. Try saying out loud, on the mic of your own life: "This is allowed to be good." Repeat it like a little prayer. Calm is not the catch. Calm is the gift.

—Real Talk Crew

Dear Surprised in a Good Way,

Growing up, we explore different things and try to make sense of things that feel unfamiliar. Being used to drama might make calm feel boring at first, but drama is not the same thing as someone actually caring about you. Real relationships are not supposed to feel like a constant fight for attention.

If someone makes you feel like you have to earn basic respect or attention, that is not healthy. My advice is to get used to things feeling calmer, even if it feels strange. You might have to be on your own for a while instead of going back to what feels familiar, but it is worth it. You deserve the best, so you have to start choosing better.

Just something to think about.

—Madison, Teen Mental Health Ambassador (Newark, NJ)

Dear Surprised in a Good Way,

What you're feeling makes sense, and it is normal. It seems like you are not used to being treated well, so now that you are, your brain is thinking, "What's the catch?" That happens to a lot of people, especially if what you have seen or heard about relationships is messy or disrespectful.

Based on everything you said, it seems like Aiden is genuine, caring, and respectful. He listens, he does not pressure you into anything, and he considers how you feel. This is what relationships are supposed to be like.

I think you feel uncomfortable because this is new to you. You might be expecting drama or someone crossing a boundary, so when it does not happen, it feels unnatural. It is okay to be a little on edge. You do not have to trust everything right away. Trust builds over time, even in good situations. Instead of waiting for things to go bad, focus on what is actually happening in the moment. I hope this helps!

—Amaris, Teen Mental Health Ambassador (Gary, IN)

Grover Cleveland Student Response by Ana Castillo

Dear Surprised in a Good Way,

I understand what you're going through. This situation is really common, and I've gone through something like this too, so I know where you're coming from. Your partner Aiden sounds like a really nice person. He sounds like a good, understanding person, and you just need to talk to him about your feelings and work the situation out.

I know it's hard trusting someone who is treating you right for the first time, but try trusting him and talking with him if you start feeling worried again. I hope for the best for both of you. I hope you're able to feel happy that you have a partner who treats you right, asks how you feel, and cares for you.

Grover Cleveland Student Response by Felicitas Odoemene

Dear Surprised in a Good Way,

No, this is not something wrong with who you are. You have to be happy with yourself without changing for other people. Every friendship or relationship you get into does not have to end up being dramatic. You just have to find the right friend or boyfriend.

When things are calm and stable, you don't have to be immediately anxious about it. Just let it be the way it should be. Everything being calm and stable is a good thing. What you should understand most is this: don't judge people by appearance. Judge them by their actions, behavior, and the way they treat you.

Love you. Be you. Be free.

Felicitas Odoemene's affirmation: "Love You. Be You. Be Free."

South 17th St. Student Response by Paris Griffiths

Dear Surprised in a Good Way,

I am sorry you are going through that. I know it is hard to trust people and open up. It is good that you have a person like Aiden.

Aiden sounds great. I think you should enjoy being with Aiden and trust him. You may get hurt sometimes, but that should not stop you from enjoying life.

Paris drew two people together under the words "trust," "healthy," and "love."

South 17th St. Student Response by Makaila Roe

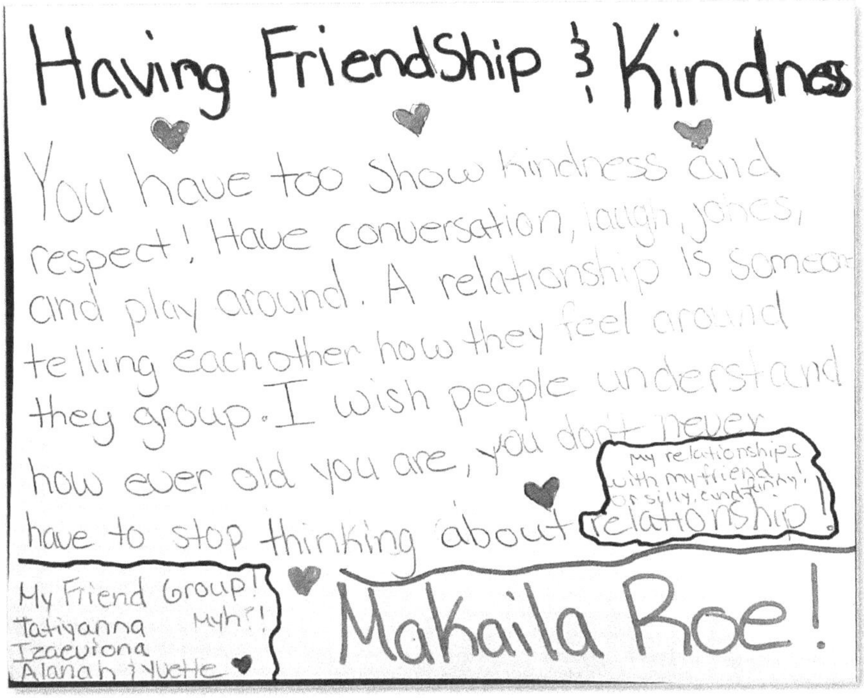

South 17th St. Student Response by Kimberly Correa

Healthy relationships are about having respect for each other and being there for one another. You should not always fight, because if you fight too much, it may not be right.

Maybe the relationship can work if both people listen and care. If it feels calm and respectful, that can be a good thing.

South 17th St. Student Response by Shavone Anthony

Dear Surprised in a Good Way: Yes, this is how a healthy relationship should feel. Anyone in a relationship should love and feel like they are heard, no matter what. You can keep that feeling by spending time with each other, going to the movies or the park, doing activities together, and communicating. Communication is key.

South 17th St. Student Response by Yvette Travis and Bridgett Wright

Real Talk Takeaway

You are allowed to have a relationship that does not require you to brace yourself. If you only know how to read storms, learning to read calm takes practice. Be patient with yourself.

After we recorded, I sat in the closet a little longer than the others. Olivia turned around in the doorway and asked, “you okay?” I said, “yeah. yeah, I’m okay.” I meant it. That was the part that surprised me.

Chapter 12 Reflection Questions

1) The *Surprised in a Good Way* letter is about a relationship that feels calm, kind, and respectful. Why might a healthy relationship feel confusing to someone who has mostly seen unhealthy ones?

2) Justin says that when you grow up watching certain kinds of arguing, calm can feel suspicious. What do you think he means by that?

3) One of the peer responses says, *"Calm is not the catch. Calm is the gift."* What are some signs that a relationship is healthy, even if it feels unfamiliar at first?

4) **Your Turn:** Finish this thought in three different ways: *"A healthy relationship should feel like..."*

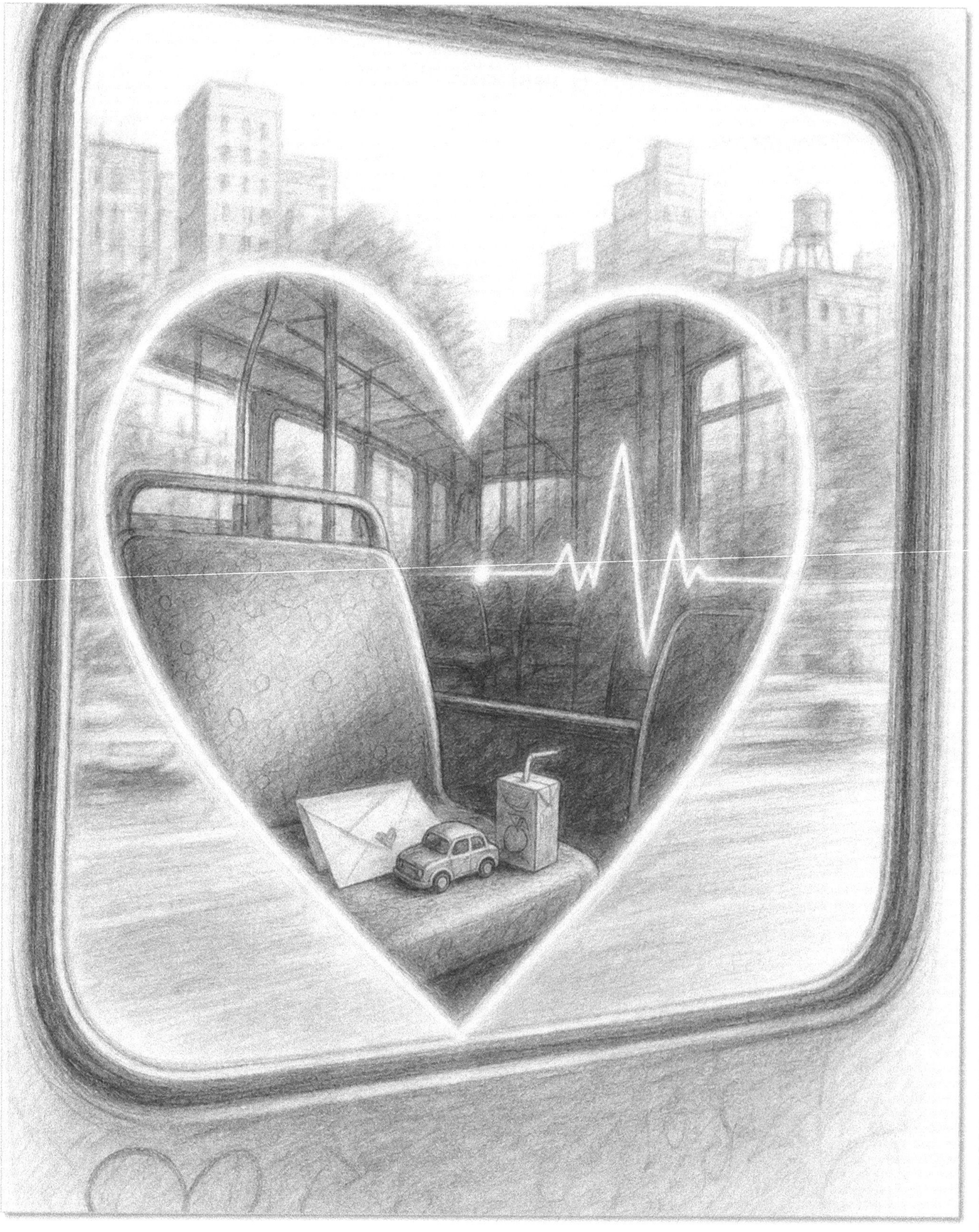

Chapter 13

Letters That Changed Everything

narrated by Tee

The contest deadline was 11:59 p.m. on a Sunday. We submitted at 7:32 p.m., because I refused to do it any later, because what if the internet hated us at 11:58.

We waited two weeks. Two slow, terrible weeks. School became long. Justin lost a Mario Kart match he should have won. Olivia drew the same butterfly twelve times in one notebook.

And then high school placement letters arrived.

I sat at the kitchen table with mine in my hand. The envelope said GREENWAY MAGNET SCHOOL. I opened it slowly. I had to read it three times to believe it.

I got in! I got in to my dream school. The one on the other side of the city. The one with the speech and debate program that goes to nationals. The one that posts pictures of their students at internships at City Hall.

I called Olivia first. She screamed. I called Justin second. He went quiet for half a second too long.

And then Olivia called me back, screaming again: "I got in!!! I got into Arts High!!!" That was her school. The local public high school of the arts. The one that has open studios and a kiln on the third floor.

I called Justin a second time. He picked up. He said, "I got my letter too."

And then he almost whispered the name of his school. A neighborhood high school. Not the one he applied to. The one with the bad reputation. The one his mom prayed he would not be placed at.

I didn't know what to say. So I assured him, "Justin, we're still us. Nothing's gonna change."

He responded with a half-hearted, "yeah."

I will remember that "yeah" for the rest of my life.

– group chat: REAL TALK CREW –

Tee: we are still us. okay? all of us.

Olivia: TODAVÍA SOMOS NOSOTROS!!! that means STILL US!!!!

Justin: okay y'all i love u. gotta go. marcus needs dinner.

Tee: love you justin.

Olivia: love you justin. con todo.

South 17th St. Student Drawing by Stephanie Kromah

🎙 **Real Talk Takeaway**

Big news can land softly for one person and heavy for another, at the same exact moment.

A promise is real. But a promise that ignores reality is just a wish in a costume.

Then we got the email from the contest. We won third place. Not first. Not the ten thousand. Third place was three thousand dollars to be split.

It was less. It was also so much. One thousand dollars each. New laptop. New paints. New gift for Justin's mom.

We screamed for about a minute. And then it got quiet. Because no amount of money was going to make our placements match.

Chapter 13 Reflection Questions

1) Tee and Olivia get into schools they are excited about, while Justin gets placed at a school with a bad reputation. How does it feel when one moment holds joy for one person and disappointment for another?

2) Tee tells Justin, *"Nothing's gonna change."* Why do you think she says that? Do you think she believes it, or does she just want it to be true?

3) The crew wins third place in the podcast contest, not the grand prize. How does this moment show that success and disappointment can happen at the same time?

4) **Your Turn:** Think of a time when your good news happened next to someone else's hard news, or the other way around. Write one thing you could say (to yourself or others) that makes space for both feelings.

Chapter 14

The Summer the Promise Got Hard

narrated by Justin

I'm going to tell you the truth. I am not going to make myself look good in this chapter. I am going to make myself look like a regular eighth grader who was scared.

Summer started fine. We won the contest. We made a flyer. We were "local podcast winners." My mom hung the article on the fridge.

But the school in my letter—I won't say the name. I'll just say what people said about it. "It's rough." "Kids fight a lot." "Don't let your guard down." The version of me that thinks he's tough laughed it off. The version of me that watches his little brother said, "Okay. Okay. I will figure it out." But the truth is, deep down, I was struggling with the news. What would the next four years look like for me?

Meanwhile Tee had a summer prep program at Greenway. Five days a week, eight to two. Buses across the city. She came home tired but charged up, like a phone someone yanked off the charger early.

Olivia had art assignments before Arts High even officially started. They sent her a packet. A whole packet. She drew on the train. She drew in her bedroom. She drew while she ate.

And me? My mom picked up extra summer shifts. So I watched Marcus. Every day. From the time he woke up until 6 p.m. when she clocked out. I love Marcus. He is the funniest six-year-old I know. But that means my day was watching cartoons, making sandwiches, refereeing his cars-on-the-rug battles, and trying not to be on my phone in front of him.

I didn't answer the group chat for two days once. Then three. Then I lied and said I had been busy when really, I had been tired in a way I didn't want to explain.

▯– *group chat: REAL TALK CREW* –

Tee: lunch tomorrow? all three of us?

Tee: justin?

Olivia: justinnnn come thrue

Justin: sorry. can't. got marcus.

Tee: okay love you. saturday?

Justin: maybe

South 17th St. Student Drawing by Nayeli Reyes Vasquez

> 🎙 **Real Talk Takeaway**
>
> Quiet from a friend is not always a mood. Sometimes it's a season. You can mean a promise and still not be able to keep it the way you imagined.

I started thinking maybe I should slow-fade. Just let it be summer. Let Tee become a Greenway kid. Let Olivia become an Arts High kid. Maybe I wasn't supposed to come with them.

I would have done that, too. I almost did. But then I got a text from Olivia I wasn't expecting.

Chapter 14 Reflection Questions

1) Justin starts answering the group chat less and less. Why do people sometimes pull away when they are stressed, tired, embarrassed, or overwhelmed?

2) Justin is watching Marcus while his mom works extra shifts, while Tee and Olivia are busy preparing for their new schools. How do responsibilities outside of school affect friendships?

3) The Real Talk Takeaway says, *"You can mean a promise and still not be able to keep it the way you imagined."* What does that mean? Have you ever had a promise become harder than you expected?

4) **Your Turn:** Write a message you could send to a friend who has gone quiet. Try to make it caring without making them feel guilty.

Chapter 15

The Text I Sent at 11:47 p.m.

narrated by Olivia

I noticed Justin going quiet. I noticed it before Tee did, but only by a few days, and only because I am a person who watches little things.

I almost didn't say anything. There is a feeling, when a friendship starts to feel thinner, that you do not want to be the one to point at the thinness. Like if nobody names it, maybe it isn't real.

But I was up late one night drawing. And I drew Justin without meaning to. Just a quick sketch. A hoodie. Earbuds. Game in his hand. And the page felt empty.

I texted him at 11:47 p.m.

I said: "Justin. I see you. I am not going anywhere. Tee is not going anywhere. We do not have to talk every day. But please do not disappear. Te quiero. That means I love you."

He texted back at 11:51 p.m.

He said: "okay." And then a minute later: "thank you O."

I cried a little, because that one okay was different from his other ones.

– group chat: REAL TALK CREW –

Justin: i think i was about to disappear. i didn't want to be a downer.

Olivia: you're not. you're tired. those are very different.

Justin: tell tee not to plan everything around me ok? i don't want to ruin her summer.

Olivia: i will tell her HALF that 😂 the other half is your job

I think about this a lot now. How easy it is to lose a person who is right there. Not because of a fight. Just because life gets thick.

I think about how, if we hadn't made this podcast, I might not have had the words to tell Justin what I told him at 11:47 p.m. I might have just sent a thumbs up emoji and gone to bed.

Real Talk made us braver. Not all the time. But more often.

> 🎙 **Real Talk Takeaway**
>
> You can love someone and still need to remind them they are loved out loud. A short text at midnight is sometimes the whole entire conversation.

Chapter 15 Reflection Questions

1) Olivia notices Justin going quiet before anyone says it out loud. What small signs might show that a friend is not okay, even if they keep saying they are fine?

2) Olivia texts Justin, *"I see you. I am not going anywhere."* Why can simple words like that mean so much during a hard season?

3) Olivia says *Real Talk* made them braver, *"not all the time, but more often."* How can practicing honest conversations in one situation help you be braver in another?

4) **Your Turn:** Write a short check-in text to someone you care about. It can be serious, funny, simple, or sweet. You do not have to send it unless you want to.

Chapter 16

The Website Idea

narrated by Tee

The three of us met on the front steps of the library on a Tuesday in August. Justin brought Marcus. Marcus brought a juice box. Olivia brought a sketchbook. I brought—say it with me—a clipboard.

I had been thinking about this all summer. About the kids who wrote in to the podcast. About all the kids who didn't write in but maybe needed to. About the kids who were rising 9th graders right now, this summer, scared.

About kids like us. About kids not exactly like us. About kids with placement letters that felt heavy.

I said it out loud for the first time on those library steps.

"What if we make a website?"

Olivia tilted her head. Justin raised an eyebrow.

"Not as the podcast," I said. "As a thing kids can come back to. A place that doesn't go away when our episode ends. Letters. Peer responses. Art. Tips. In our voices."

Justin said: "We don't have a domain."

I had one more thing to tell them. I had been interning with a youth development nonprofit called Butterfly Dreamz, Inc. They help young people build leadership skills and tell our own stories.

I had already told the staff at Butterfly Dreamz about *Real Talk.* They said if we wanted to make something for rising ninth graders, they could help us build it for real.

Olivia said: "We don't have time."

I said: "We are going to three different high schools in three weeks. Tell me one better way to leave a door open for each other and the kids coming up."

It got quiet. Marcus slurped his juice. He missed.

Justin said, "okay." But it was the good kind of okay this time.

Real Talk Website Plan

Partner: Butterfly Dreamz, Inc.

Site: www.butterflydreamz.org/realtalk

Start with three resources:

- Tee's Talk Scripts—real words for hard conversations.
- Justin's Cheat Codes—tips nobody talks about.
- Olivia's Draw It Out—drawing prompts for the high school life you want.

More can be added later! (That part made Olivia clap.)

Try This Sometime This Week

If you could leave one piece of advice for the rising 9th grader after you, what would it be? Write it in one sentence. Save it. We might use it.

Draw the school you wish existed. Stick figures are still art.

Chapter 16 Reflection Questions

1) Tee wants to create a website because a podcast episode ends, but a website can be visited again. Why might that matter for rising ninth graders or students going through a hard time?

2) Tee explains that she worked with Butterfly Dreamz, Inc. as a youth intern, and the nonprofit helps them build the website. Why is it powerful when young people help create resources for other young people?

3) The website starts with three resources: Tee's Talk Scripts, Justin's Cheat Codes, and Olivia's Draw It Out. Which one would you click first, and what would you hope to find there?

4) **Your Turn:** Add your own idea to the *Real Talk* website. Write one talk script, one cheat code, or one drawing prompt that could help someone starting high school.

Chapter 17

The Promise We Can Keep

narrated by Justin

I want to end this with the most honest thing I can say.

When Tee said "nothing's gonna change" on the phone the day we got our placement letters, I wanted to believe her. I really did. But the truth is, things changed.

Tee goes to Greenway now. She wears a school polo with a logo on it. She catches two buses to school. She loves it. She also hates it sometimes. She is making new friends. She is becoming new versions of herself. She is still my friend.

Olivia goes to Arts High. She has a sketchbook with so many drawings in it the binding is bending. She painted a mural on a wall at school. She came home from open studio one Friday and FaceTimed both of us at the same time, and we all just smiled at each other like we hadn't seen each other in a year. We hadn't. Not really. Not in the 8th-grade way we saw each other.

And me? My school is loud. Some days are hard. Some days are fine. I have new friends too. Some of them I never would have met in our old school. Marcus is in first grade now. He still thinks his big brother is famous. I'm not famous. But I'm okay.

So when people ask if the promise held—"nothing's gonna change"—I say no. That promise was wrong on purpose. We made it because we needed it that day.

But I have a better one now. We can't promise nothing will change. We can promise we will leave a light on for each other. And for the next kid coming up after us.

That is what the website is. Butterfly Dreamz helped us build it, but it still sounds like us. That is what this whole book has been too. A light on the porch for whoever needs the front steps.

If that's you—welcome. Pull up a chair (or a stack of textbooks). The mic still works. And when you finish this book, come find us online at www.butterflydreamz.org/realtalk.

Real Talk Podcast, episode you. Take one.

The Promise We Can Keep

We can't promise nothing will change. We can promise we will leave a light on.

—Tee, Justin & Olivia

Chapter 17 Reflection Questions

1) Justin says the promise *"nothing's gonna change"* was wrong, but they needed it that day. Why do people sometimes make promises they cannot fully control?

2) The crew learns they cannot promise nothing will change, but they can promise to "leave a light on." What does leaving a light on mean in a friendship, a family, or a community?

3) The book ends by inviting readers to visit the *Real Talk* website created with Butterfly Dreamz. How can a book and a website work together to help students feel less alone?

4) **Your Turn:** Write one promise you can actually keep for a friend, a classmate, your family, or yourself. Make it small enough to be real.

Sneak Peek: Real Talk Online

Built with Butterfly Dreamz, Inc. for rising ninth graders and new high school students. **Visit:** **www.butterflydreamz.org/realtalk**

SCAN ME

To start, the site has three resources. More may be added in the future, because real talk keeps growing.

Tee's Talk Scripts

Real words for hard conversations that help you avoid the drama. Use ours to get started, then write the ones that sound like you.

Justin's Cheat Codes

The tips nobody talks about. Learn some moves that make high school easier, then build your own cheat code poster to keep.

Olivia's Draw It Out

Pick up a pencil, or whatever art tool you prefer, and draw the high school experience you actually want. No art skills required, just your imagination.

We made it because starting high school should not feel like walking into the dark by yourself.

A Last Note from the Crew

Hey. You made it to the end of the book. Which means you made it through real letters from kids you don't even know, and you cared enough to keep reading.

You are already the kind of person we wrote this for.

Talk to a trusted adult. Knock on the door of a friend who got quiet. Sit with the new kid. Say the kind thing out loud. Set the boundary even if it's shaky.

We will leave a light on at www.butterflydreamz.org/realtalk.

—Tee, Justin & Olivia

Tee

Justin

Olivia

THANK YOU!

Thank you to our many young people in Newark, NJ, and Gary, IN, who helped bring this book and the Real Talk website to life through your ideas, honesty, creativity, and care. Your words helped shape the letters, responses, reflection questions, artwork, and resources in this project. This book exists because you were brave enough to tell the truth and generous enough to use your voices to help other students.

Grover Cleveland Elementary School Students (Newark, NJ)

Thank you to our Grover Cleveland Elementary School students for sharing your thoughts, questions, and real-life wisdom with us. Your voices helped us better understand what middle school students are feeling, facing, and learning as they prepare for high school. We are so grateful for the honesty, creativity, and heart you brought to this project.

Dallasia Alexander

Winnie Ayeten

Mason Barnett

Maki Beck

Zylon Bennett

Vasidiki Camara

Ana Castillo

Jahsyn Davis

Tamia Dipasalegne

Anssou Dore

Aiden Eras

Cecilia Fernandez

Tiyanna Files

Lassana Fofana

Destiny Furgess

Gabriel Garcia

Quamel Green

Jermaih Hall

Aayrin Holmes

Ah'zire Jenkins

Jonathan Jordan

Chemean Lang

Je'Nya Lowery

Jaden Loyal

Mai Lah Loyal-Murphy

Nevaeh Lucas Wynn

Serenity Nieves

Felicitas Odoemene

Jaden Parchment

Anaiyah Pressley

Taurisa Redding

Joel Rivas

Chuessy Saintime

Kyle Santos Olivo

Samuel Sawacha

Nurah Shakir

Ja'sier Terrell

Cherifa Tidjani

South 17th Street Elementary School Students (Newark, N)

Thank you to our South 17th Street Elementary School girls for contributing your ideas, reflections, and powerful perspectives. Your voices helped make this book more honest, student-centered, and meaningful for the readers who will come after you. We appreciate the courage, imagination, and care you brought to this work.

Londyn Abrams-Davis

Assiya Ameziane

Shavone Anthony

Taiyana Blue-Owens

Nakyah Boggs

Angie Bowman

Nataly Cerenegas

LeAsia Chandler

Ashley Coca

Alyssa Coleman

Kimberly Correa

Jomeily Curbelo Robles

Angeleah Darden

Naziyah Green

Anastasia Green-Lawrence

Paris Griffiths

Adia Hawkins

Treazur Hawkins

Izaevonia House

Christina Jeudy

Alanah Johnson

Trinity Jones

Stephanie Kromah

Sky Leonard

Toliya Lowe

Amy Mayorga Fierro

Melody Mendoza

Janet Oluwafemi

Kamila Osario

Nashley Placencia

Damaris Quinatoa

Evelyn Quinatoa

Nayeli Reyes Vasquez

Navaeh Robinson

Makaila Roe

Amadee Smith

Malaysia Spence

Avamarie Stevens

Nanga Tamukong

Yvette Travis

Johanna Valenzuela

Jalisa Warren

Karizza Weaver

Zyneira Weaver

Mariyah Williams

Bridgett Wright

Fathiat Yussuff

Newark, NJ Teen Mental Health Ambassadors

Thank you to our Newark Teen Mental Health Ambassadors for helping us think deeply about friendship, boundaries, conflict, support, and healing. Your responses helped make the Real Talk conversations feel honest, relevant, and rooted in what young people actually experience. You reminded us that teens are not just the audience for this work. You are leaders in it.

Fawaz Agbaje
Jalil Akinyele
Josephine Aryeh
Madison Ballobi
Sinclair Bangurah
Milo Bryant-Avila
Lutfillah Chambas
Shyann Clarke

Audrey Esteve
Nathanian Fasasi
Makayla King
Nevaeh Maldonado
Azyiah Mccray
Emerline Romeus
Lyric Scott
Tyziir Stockton

Gary, IN Teen Mental Health Ambassadors

Thank you to our Gary Teen Mental Health Ambassadors for bringing your insight, honesty, and leadership to this project. Your reflections helped strengthen the book's messages about healthy relationships, mental health, and the transition to high school. We are grateful for the way you used your voices to support students you may never meet, but who will feel seen because of you.

Madisyn Cole	*Korryne Fowler*	*Emily Matos*
Jordyn Davis	*Alexis Kemp*	*Abby Stokes*
Maliyah Dennie	*Amaris Malden*	*Nyairah Webster*

Butterfly Dreamz Staff

Thank you to the Butterfly Dreamz staff for pouring your time, talent, energy, and love into this project from beginning to end. You helped create the space where young people could share honestly, lead creatively, and turn their ideas into something real. This book and website are a reflection of your commitment to youth voice, healing, leadership, and community.

Joy Lindsay	*Michaela Dennie*	*Elijah Head*
Dominique Henderson	*Kayla Davis*	*Jontae Walters*
Leah Sampson	*Phoenyx Ojo*	*Hassane Diarrassouba*
Ashanti Castleberry	*Yaquana Williams*	*Larry Jones*

Butterfly Dreamz Board of Directors

Thank you to the Butterfly Dreamz Board of Directors for believing in the power of young people and supporting the vision behind this project. Your leadership, guidance, and commitment help make it possible for Butterfly Dreamz to create programs where youth can be heard, valued, and equipped to lead. We are grateful for the foundation you help build and protect.

Heather Lindsay	*Ashley Davis*	*Victoria Moultrie*
Tiffany Davis, Esq.	*Dr. Lynne Mock*	*Roger J. Salter*
Angela Hooper-Menifield	*Ameenah Poole*	

Our Sponsors

Thank you to our wonderful sponsors for investing in young people, youth mental health, and community-centered storytelling. Your support helped make this book and the Real Talk website possible, creating resources that students can use as they navigate relationships, school transitions, and growing up. Because of your generosity, this project can reach more young people with messages of care, courage, and support.

City of Gary, IN Health Department

Grantmakers for Girls of Color

George A. Ohl, Jr. Trust

Impact100 Essex

Legacy Foundation

PLW Partners, LLC

Turrell Fund

www.ingramcontent.com/pod-product-compliance
Lightning Source LLC
LaVergne TN
LVHW060453061126
851857LV00016B/1816
* 9 7 8 0 9 9 6 1 0 7 0 5 1 *